A GOOD DAY

KEVIN HENKES

Greenwillow Books
An Imprint of HarperCollins*Publishers*

For Chris Shelton and Marilyn Smith

A Good Day. Copyright © 2007 by Kevin Henkes. All rights reserved. Printed in the United States of America. www.harpercollinschildrens.com. Watercolor paints and brown ink were used to prepare the full-color art. The text type is 38-point Goudy Modern. Library of Congress Cataloging-in-Publication Data. Henkes, Kevin. A good day / Kevin Henkes. p. cm. "Greenwillow Books." Summary: A bird, a fox, a dog, and a squirrel overcome minor setbacks to have a very good day. ISBN-10: 0-06-114018-X (trade bdg.) ISBN-13: 978-0-06-114018-1 (trade bdg.) ISBN-10: 0-06-114019-8 (lib. bdg.) ISBN-13: 978-0-06-114019-8 (lib. bdg.) [Animals—Fiction.] I. Title. PZ7.H389Gog 2006 [E]—dc22 2005035923   First Edition 10 9 8 7 6 5 4 3 2 1

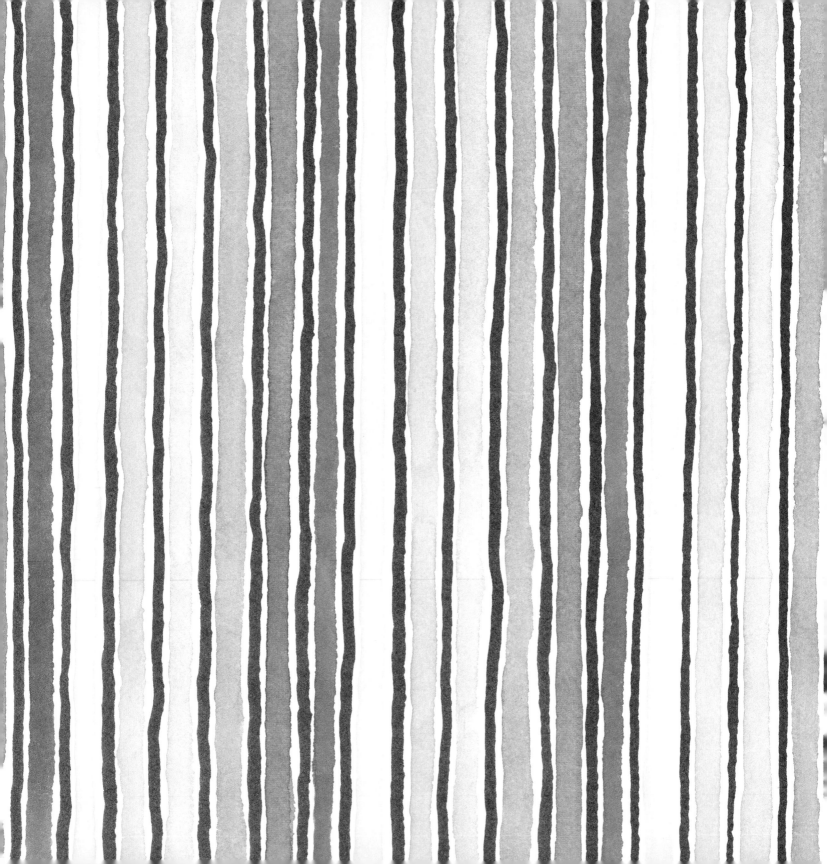

It

was

a

bad

day. . . .

Little yellow bird
lost his favorite tail feather.

Little white dog got her leash
all tangled up in the fence.

Little orange fox
couldn't find his mother.

And little brown squirrel
dropped her nut.

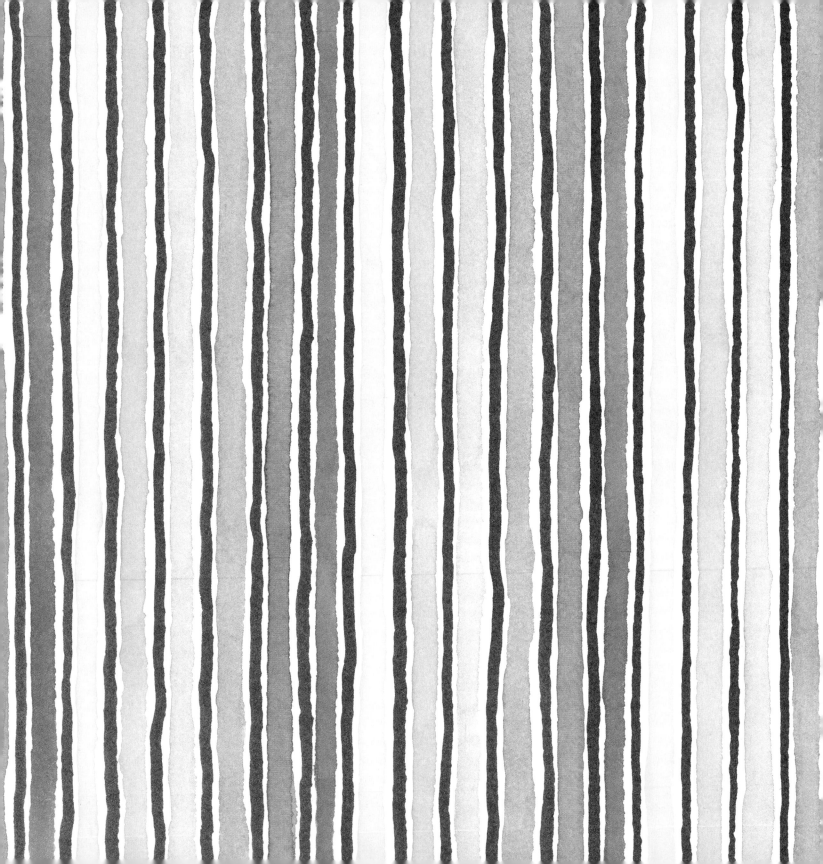

But

then . . .

Little brown squirrel
found the biggest nut ever.

Little orange fox turned around,
and there was his mother.

Little white dog worked herself free
and ran in circles
through the dandelions.

And little yellow bird
forgot about his feather
and flew higher
than he ever had before.

And there's more . . .

A little girl
spotted a perfect yellow feather,
picked it up,
tucked it behind her ear,
and ran to her mother, shouting,

"Mama! What a good day!"